"In *Sand Bodied Florida Boy*, a collection full of love and determination, Grayson writes, "to show up here, every day/an honest star." These poems articulate how much it matters to show up, to wake up, to claim your true self, despite pain and grief and loss. Can poetry save us? Maybe not, but it can help us "to realize I was never a metaphor/for wrong."
 —**Katherine Riegel**, author of *Love Songs from the End of the World*

"*Sand Bodied Florida Boy* is a lyrical journey through the labyrinth of memory and identity. This skillfully crafted chapbook explores the complex tapestry of childhood, queerness, and the enduring power of vulnerability. With "Remember all the names that brought you," Thompson invites readers to delve into a world where unwavering love and actualization intertwine. This transformative book is *what love sounds like when it comes home.*"
 —**Lexi Pelle**, author of *Let Go With The Lights On*

"With vivid imagery and fearless vulnerability, Thompson captures the transition from survival to selfhood, turning trauma into a powerful narrative of resilience and becoming. A testament to bravery and belonging, *Sand Bodied Florida Boy* is a hymn for those navigating the messy, miraculous act of existing fully."
 —**Steven Reigns**, author of *Inheritance* and *A Quilt for David*

"Sand whose nature provides a way for impressions to be made, feels like an apt metaphor for what grief and trauma do to a body. Thompson's collection asks me to sift through time whose capacity has the power to heal and also reminds us of all that we've endured. Like sand, these poems seek to name many harms endured and from that place rebuild anew as Thompson writes, *but I know what loving myself is now/ it's building a poem/ heart break by heart break*. Thompson's poems teach me that no body travels a journey unscathed and as we learn to love our grit, which these poems have, we allow ourselves and others grace and the power of the written word."
 —**Dare Williams**, poet and literary worker

SAND BODIED FLORIDA BOY

Hilary!

I'm so glad to meet
you here. Thank you for
keeping poetry alive.

SAND BODIED FLORIDA BOY

GRAYSON THOMPSON

Book and Cover Design: Cass Lintz
Cover Image by Frankie Sanchez
Courtesy of the artist
Copyright © 2025 Grayson Thompson
ISBN: 979-8-9892864-4-7

Cataloging-in-publication data is available from the Library of Congress

This book has been made possible, in part, by a grant from the Whiting Foundation

Printed in the United States of America

Foglifter Press
San Francisco, California
www.foglifterpress.com

There's a boy I know, he's the one I dream of
—Whitney Houston

for every inner child, for my niece, for me

CONTENTS

PART I: IT STARTS WITH DYING

AT MY FUNERAL: INSTRUCTIONS FOR MY EULOGY

open with:

there was always enough room
for Jack
when the Titanic sank

that Rose
was a lesson in survival

tell them I could never get over that
how it taught me to put everybody first

remind Maggie
to turn the lights off
when she leaves

teach my baby sisters
they can do hard things

but no one's meant to do hard things forever
all faith starts
with a different choice

remind them, being their
big brother was my favorite sport

tell Zac
he isn't an apology
for whoever he was before

all his parts that felt misplaced
for all the ways he tried to get it right

tell Mikey
I hope that in a Gen Z world
where he is so connected

1

that he finds someone
to show his nails to

tell Noah
he deserves a year
to be witnessed
in slow motion
that he is synonymous with my quietest parts

tell my clients
I honestly believe
there are more worse ways to live
and it's totally okay
to make a joke

or two
about wanting to die

I'll always laugh
even if it's a little true

thank Mark and Jackie
for choosing me
for showing me that love
    isn't a lightning strike
        no need to stand in a holler
        of tuning forks to hear it
        just breathing is enough

tell my aunt
declaring to me,
someone who spent decades disappearing,
that I didn't know myself
became the north star of my backbone

thank my godmother
for never forgetting to remind me
my trans ass is what a god thought of
when it created grace

tell Maggie
I wanted something remarkable
and she is what I got

I knew I was in love with her
when instead of using a spoon
        to scoop tomato sauce into a container
                        she raw dogged it with her fingers
                                        then licked them

later that night,
using those same fingers
throwing raw garlic into the compost bin,
she held my face

called me home

tell Wayne

tell my mom
there was a time
the totality of who she was

dismembered me

when I felt joy
and my life was at its highest hilarity
I'd close my eyes and wonder

what she'd think of me in these moments
when I forgot everything bad
she ever told me about myself

tell her I believed
her when she said
I'm sorry

tell my therapist
sometimes everything still hurts
I don't know why
and maybe it will always feel this way

but I know what loving myself is now
it's building a poem
heartbreak by heartbreak

it's in the way I let people feel
my soft spots
even when I do not know how to close

footnote:
here lies my brother, Wayne

we don't talk anymore
I try to remember
him like this

before everything

FOR EVERY LOST BOY

when I was a kid
I fought to keep a bead from falling
out my teddy bear's face

a purgatory
of putting a smile on

a practice
in pulling myself together

tears
evacuating eye sockets

the house was so cold
my mother bubble-wrapped
the inside with plastic

air so dry my nose bled
through the living room fort

I used to peel it
from the window

of my bedroom
reminding myself to breathe

I started a family
under my pillow
led by the short-sighted teddy bear,
a couple warrior fighters, and Tarzan

never blamed them for not waking up
when things fell apart
we all deserve a place to hide

we both should be grateful
that the socks that brought me here matched

I came here accepting being misunderstood
and there will be some things I do to protect myself

splitting a part of me
every day
to arrive here

the part that attempts assassinations
on my soft spots

it wants to fall asleep on mute
it doesn't care about beginnings

when I am apart
I need you to trust
that I am so much bigger
than blaming the family that undid me

to show up here, every day
an honest star

a conscious choice
a true cutting

you will always know me
to know me
means to ask which part I killed
to be here

before knowing your wifi password
the way you drink your tea
how you laugh in fluent magic

I will always know you
the anger that hides

in your heartburn
the wickedness that glosses

your eyes
your toes across the floor

a fierce smile
framed on my desk
reminds me that hope
isn't all that bad

love
in a real way

I heard
is like a circle

there's no easy way to start

MY THERAPIST CROSSES HIS LEG

I count the bounces of his foot
across the bow
of his posture
rhythming the silence

my body plays muffled music
and the strings break all the time

there is no noise
no feeling

above the S.O.S scars

across my chest
is an open field

I am trying
to keep the flowers

alive

DO NOT PULL LOOSE THREAD, USE THE SCISSORS

there is a dent left
in the mattress

from the accident
of waking up

half-dead statics the body
like soft kisses

a face helps me remember
the few times I felt deserved

she did not ask for that job
we do not talk

about how much I need her
she does not know

when I am sad I reel
myself memories of her smile

there are things
I did not think
about recording
there is very little left
that I answer to

that I knew a boy
in a man's body
with a scar across his head
from a time when his brain
tried to divorce him

when he wanted to die,
the most I could do was tell him
don't ever lose that brain

in my mind
I curl

inside myself
inside of myself

I do not want
to remember

how I got here
but the stitches catch on repeat

I have unraveled too
many sweaters trying
to make sense of grief

pretending does not keep the truth warm

I cover my ears
my mouth
I scream
my ribs have never known a job
like

holding

THE WARNING OF WINTER

having bipolar disorder
is more like being a polar bear

because of climate change
its average chance of catching a seal
is once in twenty hunts

being bipolar feels like those 19 times

over 300 pounds climbing
cliffs to eat bird eggs
because they don't want to die

I can climb cliffs

                                        in a manic episode

I can climb cliffs

                        because sometimes I want to die

don't be scared
don't
talk to me with a soft voice.look at me like a season finale.
stay up late, staring at the ceiling.wondering if

I'm going to be okay

a polar bear
seals slipping into the ocean
through my teeth
marveling in amazement
of all the people my mind can become

GLOSSARY OF WHITENESS I INGEST

the first word
I remember meeting

was Autumn
another word for falling

wanted to keep her name a secret
she deserved more

than people pretending
they have always known her

never held her when she was green
only crunched her
on the days she made them feel most alive

no one knew her like I did. no one
uprooted limbs to move with me in the quiet

my words were leaves
they told the stories
about the monster beneath the bed

whistled to a tune
I did not know
how to speak

a frequency of tuning forks
I couldn't use to eat

they used to kiss me like spiderwebs
I used to feel them leap

into the valleys of my brain
drop each other off at line breaks saying
we'll be back soon

when Autumn left
there was a prescription
and poem

a reminder for the poet I was
before pill time

I am still writing to bring him back

DEAD POETRY

I was raised
in the last swoon of a dinosaur

hands formed in defense
ready to fight
the other side of the womb

I saved your name as "Ma"
because when I was a kid
you couldn't stand
the noise of Boston accents
cawing
ma! ma! ma!

I do not assemble poetry
to tell the world how we collapsed

I write because all the words I heard
in school were dead

wanted posters of poems
for queer Jamaican kids everywhere

when auntie told me
you used to write
I could see all the people
that could not hear you

there is something you were trying to say
caught dead

in the way your face looks
when you sleep

when I was that little girl you tried to build
I remember at night

you would sit alone
in the living room

listening to slow songs and I would cry
so hard my baby bones grew scars

they still ache
under the low light
above my desk
when I write

when everyone is asleep
I have to erase
all the thoughts that start with

mom, I'm sorry

the only people better at lying
to themselves than queers

are whoever taught us the answer
to compassion started in how we treat others
not ourselves

if love is as love does
then the earliest thing I knew
you didn't realize you taught me

can't tell you
what it feels like

to realize I was never a metaphor
for wrong

wonder what you would think of me
in these moments

when I forget everything
your fear ever told me about myself

come in
keep your shoes on

there is over twenty years of stepping
all over myself here

there is no more damage
that you can do

I meant to go missing
I got here by accident

I wanted to create something
but never knew where to put my hands

all of this noise
the messiness
this is my body

and if I do not let go
of never being loved
in all the ways I needed to

I will kill everything

PART II: THE TRAUMA DID IT

...instead of wanting more, sometimes I just made myself want even less. Sometimes I made myself believe that I wanted nothing, not even food or air. And if I wanted nothing, I'd just have to turn in to a ghost. And that would be the end of it...
—Kevin Wilson

GROWING INTO MY CLOTHES

and the way change
washes through

slipping between
the worn pockets

I was asked, once,
where my happiness went

and I didn't know
how to say I lost it in some jeans

in the trauma
a gasping pasture

willing a single rain cloud for its tears
but that cloud is wearing a raincoat

due to fear of falling apart

I'm the kid in the field
covering my ears
from them wailing
for protection

it looks like me
the way I swallow hearts

throw up all their bad parts
so that other people can sleep
better at night

raise your hand
if you are afraid
of the dark

I am

even most when the lights are on
maybe that is the only way
people like us still believe

in childhood
when we had the ability to see
the world
naked and asking
all the tough questions like:

who would have thought topic would have a C at the end?
if I was born before you, would I be older than you?

is my father, a father?

honest
not earnest

not trying and failing
honest
like you really meant it that time

WHEN YOU USED TO SAY MY NAME LIKE THAT

building a relationship with someone is

a shuddering phone line
wrapped in a hurricane
holding between two poles
across a cornfield the length of the sunset

delicate

as it swings over
the riptide of stalks reach up
like christmas trees touching god

the line snaps
like gospel

the words left unsaid fall
hard into the roots
of ocean golden green

I swear

every time a husk breaks
I still hear you say
you love me

THROWING FIREBALLS AT CLOSET DOORS IN THE
GREATEST PLACE ON EARTH

Joe was from Queens
and wore leather jackets in Florida

his writer aesthetic, he was too cool
with wavy slicked back black hair
and burnt butter-honeyed skin

we didn't plan it
here we were

looking for each other
in a sea of technicolor beads

standing next to a sign that read
BIG ASS
BEER

there was more than one
we started playing gopher
with neon signs

crowded bodies parted
he looked like
when you take a hard left
with a fresh pizza on the seat

bent on one side
with sauce dripping out
steaming

he had a fourth of a bottle of Fireball
lightly swaying from his hand
and a sleepy smile

two Florida writers drunk on Bourbon Street
he said to make sure we write about this for class

pulls some weed out of his pocket
told me he became friends over a joint
with some sex workers the night before

I was in town on a trip with a closeted partner
and their best friend who didn't know
drunk with Joe, looking at them
having an existential conversation
with a huge Southern white man named MEAT

the thoughts crawled
out the back of my mind, unrestricted:

I was alone and hated this part of my life

in the backlit alley with Joe
staring at my circuit partied reflection in streams of piss
I didn't feel so empty

we drunkenly dragged each other to his hotel
the rich people ushering in and out

with nice clothes and nice cars
there were different kinds of beads
around these women's necks

the two of us brown-skinned
in street clothes

linguine arms across shoulders
looking more alive than they ever felt

I left Joe at the steps
a lifeboat abandoned

I submitted a piece to the professor
it was returned murdered in red

I should have wrote:

I was a gender-confused and angry guy
fist fighting with my face

and that dude took as much as he gave

in an affair with a human closeted in shame
in a life where I was remnants of eraser rubber

that trip was an ongoing series
of me trying to forget
myself with alcohol

I only really remember Joe
parting the sea of sweaty drunks with Fireball
a guy I only knew through black words on white paper

because only writers
know how to hurt
like that

A GOD OR A DREAM, SOMETHING TO LET GO OF
(thank you Neck Deep, for being my quarantine preacher, and for "A Part of Me")

my astigmatism scatters
the light
of your body

you hit
planets aligning in slow motion
each graze makes it hard to breathe

without it
I feel the cold
of infinite stars

I hope you're somewhere
in the corners
of my consciousness

softening where the shame lives
hope you can see I'm stumbling
toward you

knees first
waiting to collapse
palms spread like a tome

spine cracked open
praying
for you
to reach
through the inside

I found this hope
in a punk rock band
an acoustic singer
voice rugged like bedsheets

watched as the people sang back
through the distance between them

the preacherman sang
lost his voice
holding back tears
thinking of a girl

heard the congregation
fill in all the things
he couldn't say to her

I am the boy in the sea
of drowning voices
behind the guitar strings

close my eyes
raise my hands

this is the only time I'll let you shoot me

in the back of some bar
in some place I've never been

staring at the back of your head
crying at the halo

A LANDSCAPE PAINTED WITH EVERY SAD THING

(with gratitude to Rhina Espaillat for her poem "On the Impossibility of Translation")

stretching my heart
the length of a grenade field

and breathing   has me looking like a mason jar

of fireflies dying

wheezing wingtips
carcass
and burnt-out buds.

I knew pain

way before I knew myself

one
by
one

a   jump

from the mending wall

into the oblivion of my bones
where the stars sleep soundly lulling

love me
love me
love me

next to sleep, depression is another place

where I lose

myself to the ▮▮▮
to the wandering mind   of

restlessness

pulled the pins

if the two
were to collide tell them

separated

the beehives and

the oceans from

god

I

walked

on the

melting sun

dew drops

of myself

b
r
e a
king

I tried

took three-word breaths
peeled back my top and bottom eyelids
opened my mouth ithe length of the sunset,
    one day I will believe that the world
    is not made of tsunamis
    bowling me over.
    I will write it down over and over:

I believe,
I believe

until it translates into the sound of my voice
folding the earth into the syllable of un-
done

there you will find me speaking in fluent song

29

AT 9:30 MY WOMAN BECAME SIX POUNDS REMOVED

you are and you are
not all the yous you have been
relish this. breathe. mourn.

remember all the names
that brought you

all the in-betweens
what they carried

each syllable they ate
and how unsure it felt to be

a man

PART III: SIGNAL ME AN APOLOGY

my foster mom, my second mom,
says throughout time, as we grow and change, we are going through:

"the sifter"
—Jaclyn Saltzman

PHEROMONE LAWN

after another 10-hour workday in florida,
we camped on someone's front lawn

sweat-kissed bodies
drinking four lokos

summer nights where I lost myself
to joy

my friend threw up in the bushes
half body/half bush
I watched
as she danced on the ground
to her song snatching water in the air

one of the first times love
struck me dead

how did she remember it?
we don't talk anymore

half etching/half person
half memory/half miracle-we-made-it

sprinklers trapped us
in the tent
drowning
swimming ourselves invincible

I never went back to sleep

DOES GOD LIVE IN ATTICS?

this used to be a poem
but it didn't sound like me anymore

I hoped you would hear my bones
hum to the key of release
and maybe, you'd sing along

maybe I'd stop crying in my sleep
stop running into the darkness
across the ceiling at night

when I wrote that poem,
I meant to say
you're my home, you're my home

when I love someone, I hold on
to each rock that forms in my stomach
from all the bad parts

they leave

I throw up boulders

wail into the pristine toilet
there's a monster
that sings back
behind my eyes and in the walls

about the twenty years spent holding
every grieving sound hostage
in my throat

THE RAIN AND BEAUTIFUL THINGS THAT PURGE

this story was true
there was a girl out there that binged
on her mom's leftover projections

I wanted to spike her with sunshine
make her blackouts look like dawn

I felt like a dead labyrinth
of word search puzzles
only kept here by scars
binding my book body

I, like the girl from another life,
who vomited up all of her
lost loving myself
in my alphabet soup bloodstream

thought if I bent back my head far enough,
the slice of the pen would fill the missing words in

I told her we both were gonna get tattoos
that said we're gonna practice not blowing up
our reflections
there's enough bad luck
out there without our help
and our mirrors deserve better treatment than that

she once asked, *write me a poem about loving my body*

please.
I need it
or about not losing control
or over thinking about overeating

she found the poem
I do not know if she found it in the dark
at the end of everything she let out
knowing her, she wrote her own way into the light

there will always be something there
beyond the color-by-number of constellations

to dress our infinity arms like Christmas trees
when we choose to reach for hope

I am still learning how to wear the cape
I am not an answer messenger
I am still learning

her smile reaches both ends of hello
and that is what love sounds like
when it comes home

FOR EVERY FAILED FRIENDSHIP

I meant to show up like this and surprise you
to be both selfish and loving
learning how to make sense of compersion
an apology they don't have syllables for yet
it took me so long

to ask how you were when I was busy
becoming
cellular whispers
across places neither of us could fit
infinitely large
like the first broken promise we made

to always be around
I was so proud
when I finally forgot the sound of your voice
the notes of your laugh
to lose the chasing
some people grow

so apart their insides change
the first place you notice is in their smile
the last time I saw yours
I was trying to make sense of resentment
in all the things you didn't say
and that wasn't fair

an impossible thing to fill
I wrote this to remind myself
that love creeps back in
when you remember
I wrote this because I never forgot
to leave the door open

to crack everything
splinter so deep
when I pull
all the synonyms for grief bleed out
I've missed you

like the first good poem I wrote
only one I could never put to bed
did I have to know every version of you
to mean every word I ever said?
all your breaks
left rivers in my five-alarm chest speaker

I hope they brought you some rest
in another life
you were louder than everything
than all the hard things
a complication of circumstance
a distant lullaby of sea foam kissing sand

THE CALLER YOU ARE TRYING TO REACH IS NOT AVAILABLE

your voice sounds like oxygen

you say hello
with an emphasis on hell

your lips hug each syllable
like a southern summer haze

I always can find a poem in your name
I fear,
        I know,
                    I'm not sure

how exactly your hair looks now
when it liquids through sunlight

I tell you it is funny how your voice became a woman
I tell you how me being me is hard

I believe you when you say you know
like you have been behind the curtain the whole time
when the Wizard did not make me a boy

I remember the tent
and the Four Lokos

and the you I remember
and the you I no longer know

PART IV: ARRIVING ON PURPOSE

CEASE FIRE SANDWICHES FOR THE REVERE BEACH BOY

I grew up with mortal incarnations
of wickedness ██████████

██████████
████ hands
choked the difference out of me
a derivative for queerness
an amalgamation of manhood
called petty ████████
thought small and smaller
sunk into the gap ████████ wall and the mattress
made love to dust

████████ my youth ██████████
an icy hill
sliding ████ homegrown heartache
██ birth ██ hunting
purple fringed photographs
muted ████
stabbing odd
angled birthday cake
pink raincoat on a pony
holding pumpkins
the weight of church confessions

it wouldn't be pathetic ████ if there is a god
anything bigger
than us with control
the adult in the room for adults ████████ the answer
some of my biggest shame is ████████
in the memory of ████████
it started more wars than I can count

I am here now
and I mean it
signal me an apology
I didn't know how long this would take

JUNIPER POPLAR

I knew a guy who lost over 100lbs
by running away
from himself

he taught me
start small
like a building

eventually turn the world over
with my feet

the first block hit me
like an alabaster whale

the dark wooded bridge
reminded me of how fast ghosts can run

I wrapped myself in swisher sweets and smoke

the burn
makes everything okay

in the end
when my time comes

bury me in a coffin of compliments
because
even what
you hate
deserves to rest
        my bones
          are made of moon ashes

    let the earth swallow me whole

I've always
wondered

what it felt like to move a tide

VERBAL PARAPHASIA FOR GRATITUDE

thank you
rhymes with intensive care unit

where I was born
a premature second coming
the first
my brother
a narcissistic star

my neighbor
operated 911 dispatch
told me in the stairwell

mother's day
was one of the busiest days
of the year

she rhymes with psalm
I remember the way she'd call in 23,27,91
before the at of her email address
I would tell her

Ma,
you don't need prayers
in job applications

her resume
a hymn filled with synonyms
for mercy

I was taught God punishes
everyone
the best and worst in us

my niece
tells me to pray about my stress
asks if hormones can heal
questions if freedom is something you wish for

I said yes

told her that love is
the freest thing
you don't have to do anything
be anyone
to receive it

thank god
I have lived through enough lifetimes
to teach lessons I finally know are true

verbal paraphasia is a cognitive symptom
disorganized speech

why kaleidoscopes and crash landings sound like they go together
why my partner looks at me like
I put my name on backwards

she'll fill in the gaps anyway
mostly with honey,
sometimes with tears

says I can find a poem in any word
a penchant for breaking

some people believe violent dreams
are predictors of a manic episode

I'd like to think it's my more honest half
trying to touch grass again

because the other guy is committed
to listening to the saddest sentences

these gratitudes came
before I began mixing up weather and better

before thinking I was an empty terminal
arriving tired
tossed and green

there is something more
intimate and more terrifying than surrender
it lives in believing that we deserve to feel good

I am filled with hope
despite popular belief

to live in a world
of children eating their monsters for breakfast
who know without question
that drag is the future
and none of this life was made to make sense

this infinite of becoming
undoing the squareness
of the ways I have been caged

spent years having my grace muffled
in unready mouths
like gravel
rhymes with grief

the grief
bent me into accommodations
I was never made to make

there are no more apologies
for the ways I have been broken

you can find all my love
in the back of a writing desk drawer

opening all the things I could not say

made a legacy of eating life's lemons whole
open my mouth

see the seeds growing
from the mess I made

it took so much sour to get here
it would mean the most to me

if you never forgot
everything I carried
all the pulp and all the pain

born yellow
it's understandable
all the people who could not look at me

here is a story
that nobody heard
we were already born with perfect parts

I was already born with perfect parts

SAND BODIED FLORIDA BOY

it is rude
to be told
you come from nowhere

swamp
and sweaty ocean

eight million people
drinking water
from the Everglades

you do not know
what it is like
to be baptized
in dinosaur bones

called my mother
through the silence of palm trees
dragged myself from the marsh

hummed myself humid
hailed every word
after a jehovah witness doorknock
throat orange hurricane
spun me into a hermit

tried to kill my queerness
on the porch

ten-legged behind a rearview
shell of a child
eating dark-worded bees whole
in a choir of echoes

send my ashes to Fort Lauderdale beach
complete the promise to Ma
that I'll come back soon

never knew how to mean it
didn't mean to go missing with each grain
there's an audience
of every sad thing in my bedroom

open the window
shake the sand out

I want to be
back in my body

PERPENDICULAR TOWN

legacy
is defined as something we get
from the past
here it is

synonymous with trauma
adjacent to carrying
the kitchen sink and my family

in one hand
with the other
trying to arrive here empty handed

I am no longer terrified
of what the pain would do
if I brought it all out

on purpose

I am so big up close
papier-mâchéd with possibility

you won't believe how long this took

FOR ANYONE HOLDING THEIR BREATH

this is a love poem
for all boys

who have never been told
they were beautiful

for people who do not know
they smile in their sleep

for the adult children who can't call home

this is a page
in a story that places bets
on the weight of bobcats

heavy handed with softness
each pound a metaphor for

you are not alone

I want to tell you
in the same century grief
was first spoken
so was breviary

a word for hymn

and this is a truth,
god honest

some of us
have applied for the vacancy
of being alive
since before we were born

our resumes
half spent lifetimes
never making it to the top
even if we stopped ourselves from being
propelled by everything that hates us

I do not know who interviewed you
but in that round,
the one where you painted yourself a crisis
someone should have told you

the job responsibilities
were never to hold it all in

ACKNOWLEDGEMENTS

I want to give a huge shoutout to the following literary magazines for creating a home for some of my poems in this collection, in one form or another: Poetry Online, Cleaver Magazine, High Shelf Press, Belletrist, Cathexis Northwest Press, Foglifter Press, and Backbone Press. Thank you for keeping poetry alive and choosing my work to be part of your literary stories.

I want to share specific gratitudes for:

my therapist: what a return on investment

my friends: wherever you are, thank you for being here

V: for your meticulous edits and late-night cackles

frankie: your deep mirroring and book cover art

suanny barales: because venmo is not enough

buddy wakefield: for that Christmas and our writer family

my family: look at this beautiful thing I made

gabby fluke-mogul: for every median surfed

exhibit b: salons and taco bell and bad pizza

marguerite elisabeth scott—
    I love you in every imagination

Grayson Thompson [he/him] is a Black, Jamaican-American, queer trans-gender cowboy poet who moonlights as a therapist. A mouthful, Grayson is Foglifter Press' 2024 Start A Riot! Chapbook Prize Winner with *SAND BODIED FLORIDA BOY* and Winner of Write Bloody Publishing's 2024 Jack McCarthy Book Prize for his forthcoming debut full-length collection, *A CONGREGATION OF ALLIGATORS* (September 2025). Grayson has been featured in Cathexis Northwest Press, *Foglifter*, *Cleaver* (nominated for Best of the Net Anthology), *Poetry Online*, and other homes for poetry. As a performer for the Exhibit B Literary Variety Show in Kansas City during the 2024 AWP Conference, he was able to open for the badass Kansas City Poet Laureate, Melissa Ferrer Civil, and a hero—the amazing Donika Kelly. Grayson is a teaching assistant for poet Buddy Wakefield's Writer's Anonymous where he supports emerging and established word assem-blers. A wanderer, he lives in Northern California where you can find him hiking, curating salad recipes, and in awe of the ocean. He chooses mad-ness, honest and full-hearted. He hopes you can find some in his poems.

Find him on IG: @graysonwritespoems

Frankie Sanchez is a writer, poet, and freelance graphic designer. A coffee-infused doodler, member of the LGBTQIA+ community, and a landscape of pillow practice who imagines his work might one day be folded complexly into novel paper planes. He's a 2024 Finalist and Honorable Mention for Write Bloody's Jack McCarthy Book Prize and the sole member of the Ipsum Lorem Yacht Club.

You can learn more at fkafrancis.com.

Rooted in the San Francisco Bay Area, Foglifter Press is a platform for LGBTQ+ writers that supports and uplifts powerful, intersectional, and transgressive queer and trans writing through publication and public readings to build and enrich our communities as well as the greater literary arts.

Eye the margins.

www.foglifterpress.com

This book was set in PT Serif and Optima.

www.ingramcontent.com/pod-product-compliance
Lightning Source LLC
Jackson TN
JSHW072047150525
84567JS00016B/77